Animals

Pandas

by Nick Rebman

FOCUS READERS

FOCUS READERS

www.focusreaders.com

Focus Readers is distributed by North Star Editions:
sales@northstareditions.com | 888-417-0195

Produced for Focus Readers by Red Line Editorial.

Photographs ©: DennisvandenElzen/Shutterstock Images, cover, 1; Hung Chung Chih/Shutterstock Images, 4, 15, 16 (bottom right); irakite/Shutterstock Images, 7, 16 (bottom left); Fernan Archilla/Shutterstock Images, 9; TamasV/Shutterstock Images, 11, 16 (top right); leungchopan/Shutterstock Images, 13; ssguy/Shutterstock Images, 16 (top left)

ISBN
978-1-63517-853-1 (hardcover)
978-1-63517-954-5 (paperback)
978-1-64185-157-2 (ebook pdf)
978-1-64185-056-8 (hosted ebook)

Library of Congress Control Number: 2018931103

Printed in the United States of America
Mankato, MN
May, 2018

About the Author

Nick Rebman enjoys reading, drawing, and traveling to places where he doesn't speak the language. He lives in Minnesota.

Table of Contents

Pandas

Pandas are bears.

They have black **fur**.

They have white fur.

A panda has two **ears**.

A panda has two eyes.

A panda has four legs.

ear
eye
leg

Behavior

Pandas go up in trees.

Pandas live alone.

Pandas live in **forests**.

They find food to eat.

forest

Food

Pandas eat **bamboo**.

Bamboo is a kind of grass.

Pandas eat all day.

bamboo

Pandas are big.

They can live for 20 years.

Glossary

bamboo

forests

ears

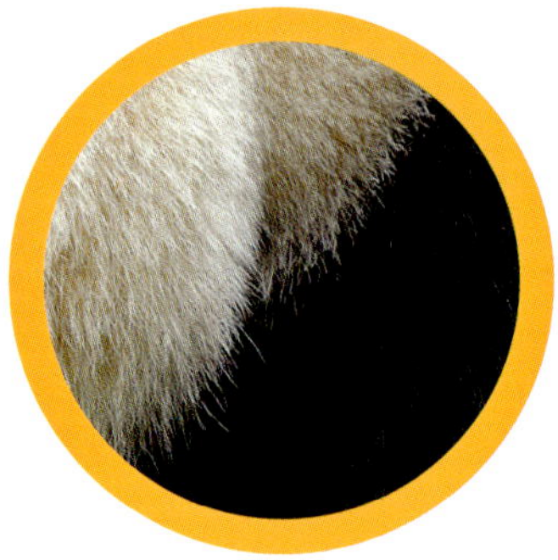

fur

Index